WESTMINSTER SCHOOLS

SMYTHE GAMBRELL
LIBRARY

PRESENTED BY

Margaret McCune
in memory of
Mrs. James C. Malone

1986.
Cate Candler

The Best
Present Is Me

BATH CURTAIN:

BATHROOM TILE:

LIVING ROOM CHAIR:

WOODEN HALL FLOOR:

BATHROOM RADIATOR:

POTHOLDER:

MAP OF NEW YORK CITY:

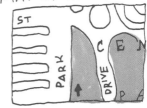

SWISS CHEESE and DEVILED EGGS:

EDDIE'S SHIRT:

OMA'S NEEDLES and YARN:

GRANDPA'S GLASSES:

LIVING ROOM RUG:

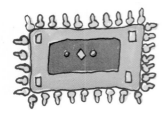

BATHROOM FLOOR:

GRANDPA'S TIE:

DINING ROOM
TABLECLOTH:

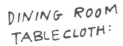

TEAPOT, CUP and
SAUCER:

LOBBY FLOOR:

The Best
Present Is Me

WRITTEN AND ILLUSTRATED BY
Janet Wolf

OMA'S DRESS:

Harper & Row, Publishers

HALL WALLPAPER:

HALL STAIRCASE:

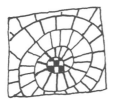

NOTEBOOK PAPER:

with special thanks to
Laura and Harriett

Library of Congress Cataloging in Publication Data
Wolf, Janet, 1957–
    The best present is me.

    Summary: A small girl travels to New York City
with her parents to celebrate her grandmother's
birthday, but along the way loses the present she
has made.
    [1. Grandmothers—Fiction.   2. Birthdays—Fiction.
3. Presents—Fiction.   4. Lost and found possessions —
Fiction.   5. New York (N.Y.)—Fiction] I. Title.
PZ7.W81914Be 1984   [E]   82-48853
ISBN 0-06-026583-3
ISBN 0-06-026584-1 (lib. bdg.)

For Mom, Dad, and Marion

On Sundays we go to visit Oma and Grandpa in New York City. Today is Oma's birthday. I take out my best crayons (not the cracked ones in the cookie tin) and make a big picture of me. I lie still on a piece of paper, and Mommy traces my outline. I color it in. I hope Oma will like it—the arms came out a little funny. Daddy is honking the horn, so I roll up the picture and run outside to the car.

We drive for a long time through little towns
and over the big bridge. From my window I
can see the whole city. We sing "Knick
Knack Paddywhack" and count the red cars.
The houses are close together and the
streets crisscrossed. Oma and Grandpa
live on a hill up the block from the river and
the park.

78

79

20

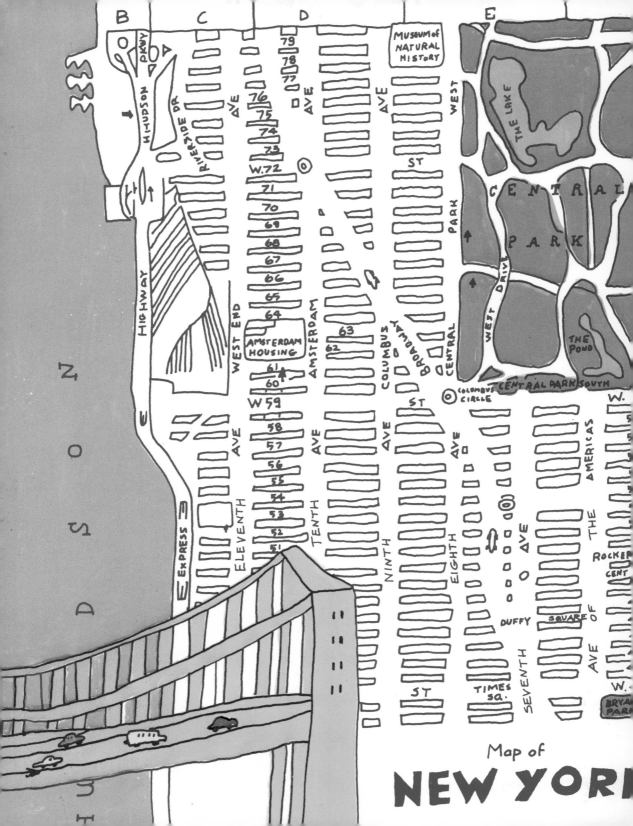

Map of
NEW YORK

I ring the bell to let Oma and Grandpa
know we are here.

Then I press the button for the elevator. "Good morning," says Vito, the elevator man. He knows me. It is hot, so I take off my mittens and scarf and hat and give them to my mother. I put down Oma's present.

We go up to the fourth floor. We say thank you and get out. The door creaks.

The hall smells like meat loaf cooking.
When I walk across the landing, I can lean
over and stare way down to the bottom.
If I look too long I get dizzy.

Oma and Grandpa live in 4G.

"Hello, Schatzi!" Oma hugs me tight. She has soft arms. She smells like soap and fresh linen.

"Happy Birthday, Oma!" I smile.

Grandpa gets up from his chair. He checks his pocket watch. I run up and give him a big hug and kiss.

I walk down the long, long hallway. The floor is wood, and my steps sound like tap dancing. All along the wall is an enormous mirror. There are lots of doors. Two gentlemen rent rooms from Oma. I have never seen them. I imagine one is fat and likes to read. The other is an opera singer. I turn the white shiny knob of the bathroom door and go in.

ROOMER #1

ROOMER #2

A little later I go to the kitchen to see what's for lunch. Cheese, deviled eggs, pickles, ham, bologna, roast beef, and pea soup. A basket is filled with warm toast straight out of the toaster. A kettle is squealing. Oma is using the potholder I made her!

The long table is set with fancy white china.
I get a special seat next to Oma. Eddie sits
next to me. He eats ham with his fingers.

1. GRANDPA   3. DAD   5. OMA   7. EDDIE
2. UNCLE   4. MOM   6. AUNT   8. ME

The grown-ups talk for a long time. Eddie
and I play Giant Steps. He gets to do all the
fancy steps. I get the baby steps!

BANANA STEP   BABY STEP   UMBRELLA STEP   BABY STEP   FROG LEAP   BACKWARDS BANANA STEP

RABBIT HOP   BABY STEP   GIANT STEP   BABY STEP   SIDE STEP   I DON'T WANT TO PLAY

Then we play post office at Grandpa's
special desk. It is big and wooden, with a
matching chair on wheels that spin. I am the
mailroom clerk. I use a rubber stamp to
mark envelopes, and a sponge to wet the
sticky part. I make a birthday card for
Oma. It says, "A special gift waits for you
in the bedroom." Eddie is the messenger.
He makes the deliveries.

I sit on Grandpa's lap. Oma opens Eddie's present. It's a handmade model plane. Oma loves it.

Then Oma opens my letter and smiles. "Thank you, sweetie. I can't wait to see the present."

I jump up to get it. I go down the long hall
with the mirror, past the roomers' rooms to
the back room where our coats and hats
and mittens and scarves and presents lie in
a heap on the bed.

I search, but there is no picture from me.

If I work fast maybe I can make another
one. But Oma comes in. When she looks at
me she understands. She puts her arm
around me.

"You know the best present is right here."
And she gives me a big hug.

The doorbell rings. It's Vito!